MR. TICKLE
and the Dragon

originated by Roger Hargreaves

Written and illustrated by Adam Hargreaves

MR. MEN   **LITTLE MISS**

Mr. Men and Little Miss™ and © THOIP (a Sanrio company).

PSS!
PRICE STERN SLOAN
An Imprint of Penguin Group (USA) Inc.

ISBN 978-0-8431-3278-6   20 19 18 17 16 15 14 13

Mr. Tickle was having a very good day. Twenty-one people well and truly tickled. A very good day indeed.

But when he arrived home, he could not believe his eyes.

"I can't believe my eyes," he said to himself. "Somebody has burned down my house!"

Mr. Tickle's house was gone. All that was left was a smoking, charred pile at the end of his garden path.

There was more smoke rising from the end of the lane.

Mr. Tickle set off to investigate.

The smoke was coming from Mr. Funny's shoe car. Or rather, it had been his car, but all that remained was a burned shoelace.

Mr. Tickle could see another spiral of smoke in the distance.

This time it was Mr. Clever's house, and very nearly Mr. Clever by the look of him!

"I just got out in time," said Mr. Clever. "There can only be one culprit. It must have been a . . ."

But Mr. Tickle did not wait to hear what it must have been. He had spotted the signs of another fire and was determined to follow the trail.

It was a long trail which led from Mr. Chatterbox's burned-out phone booth to Farmer Field's burned-down barn, and on through wilder, bleaker land, up into the mountains. Soon it began to get dark, but Mr. Tickle continued to climb higher and higher.

Darkness had fallen when he saw a bright light. In the distance, there was a cave emitting a red glow.

Suddenly Mr. Tickle did not feel very brave. Suddenly he wished he had stayed to hear what Mr. Clever had had to say.

Mr. Tickle decided to wait there until the morning. He curled up under a bush and wrapped his arms around himself three times to keep warm.

Mr. Tickle fell into a surprisingly deep sleep and the sun was up when he was woken by the rustling of the bush.

Mr. Tickle opened an eye.

The bush rustled again.

"I know you're in there," rumbled a very deep voice. **"Come on! Show yourself!"**

Mr. Tickle cautiously poked his head through the top of the bush and stood blinking in the bright sunlight. He was quite unprepared for the sight that met his eyes.

He was standing face-to-face with a dragon!

A huge dragon at that.

A huge dragon with smoke curling from his nostrils.

Mr. Tickle gulped.

"Hello," said Mr. Tickle in a tiny voice.

"I'm going to give you thirty seconds to give me a good reason why I shouldn't burn you to a crisp," bellowed the dragon, **"and then I'm going to burn you to a crisp!"**

Mr. Tickle gulped a second time.

Mr. Tickle needed to think fast. He realized his arms were hidden. Quick as a flash he sent one of his extraordinarily long arms snaking through the bushes and under the dragon's belly.

Mr. Tickle flexed his fingers and hoped beyond everything that dragons are ticklish.

The dragon instantly crumbled into a giggling, laughing tangle on the ground.

"Ha! Ha! Ha!" roared the dragon.
"Hee! Hee! Hee!" wheezed the dragon.
"Ho! Ho! Ho!" boomed the dragon.
"Stop it! Stop it!" he cried.

"I'll stop tickling if you promise to stop burning things," said Mr. Tickle.

"Anything! I'll promise anything!"
pleaded the dragon.

Mr. Tickle stopped tickling and looked the dragon squarely in the eye.

"What you need to learn," said Mr. Tickle, "is to put your fire breathing to good use. You should be using your extraordinary skills to make people happy. I'll show you."

The dragon lay down on the ground and Mr. Tickle hopped on his back. Then the dragon shook out his great wings and took off, circling high over the mountains and swooping down to the distant valleys.

They flew lower and lower, passing over barns and cottages.

"Look!" cried Mr. Tickle. "It's Little Miss Splendid's house. I have an idea for your first good deed!"

Mr. Tickle and the dragon stood beside Little Miss Splendid's swimming pool.

"It is too cold today to swim in Little Miss Splendid's pool," said Mr. Tickle. "Do you think you could do anything about that?"

The dragon thought for a moment.

Then he took a deep breath and breathed out through his nostrils. Flames licked across the surface of the swimming pool. In no time at all the pool was steaming.

Little Miss Splendid was delighted. Mr. Tickle, the dragon, and Little Miss Splendid had a very enjoyable swim.

In fact, the dragon had a very enjoyable day.

He melted the ice on Mr. Bump's path, and Mr. Bump couldn't have been happier, as most mornings he usually slipped and bumped his head.

He warmed up Mr. Forgetful's cup of tea, which he had made at breakfast time and forgotten to drink. Mr. Forgetful was delighted. He doesn't normally get to drink hot tea!

And Mr. Greedy was very impressed when the dragon cooked fifteen sausages all at once.

By the end of the day, the dragon had a big glowing smile across his face.

"Do you know what?" he boomed cheerfully. **"I feel really good!"**

Mr. Tickle grinned and then he reached out his extraordinarily long arms . . .

. . . and tickled the dragon!

"And now I do, too!" he laughed.